Human beings and dogs have enjoyed a close, collaborative relationship for millennia. Dogs are our loyal companions, our helpers when we have physical and psychological needs, and our partners in a variety of fields of work. But what is their perspective on this relationship? How do they see us and the world around them? Helen Pasanen has given us one possible answer through the eyes of Teddy, a friendly Cairn Terrier who loves his mistress and is ever curious about the world around him. Through Teddy's interactions with his human friends and his environment, she offers a vision of a world in which gratitude, wonder, and assuming the best of others are the rules. At this moment in time, Teddy's appeal to "our better angels" is all the more attractive.

—Dr. Peter Farrugia
author and associate professor
History and Social and Environment Justice Programs
Research and Academic Centre West
Wilfred Laurier University
Brantford, Ontario, Canada

Teddy's Dog Diary is a brief look at everyday life as seen through the eyes of an adorable Cairn Terrier. As Teddy shares his thoughts and encounters with humans and nature, we get a different perspective into things we may otherwise take for granted. The author, Helen Pasanen, has a unique way of capturing the reader's attention and challenges us to think about our relationship to God, our environment, and each other. I highly recommend this book for older children, but I also think that adults would enjoy it just as much. I found *Teddy's Dog Diary* not only inspiring but also entertaining and informative! Thank you, Helen, for blessing us with your wonderful, God-given gift!

—Cheryl Daly
retired teacher
Brantford, Ontario, Canada

I really enjoyed this book. The author was able to take the reader into the wonderful world of a dog. I would recommend this book to my friends.

—Erica Wilson
ten years old
Kitchener, Ontario, Canada

I thoroughly enjoyed reading about Teddy's many adventures during his holiday with Art and Helen. He brought a smile to our faces each day as he would stand at the fence and let Ron know that he was there, anxiously waiting for his treat.

—Yvonne Porter
Helen and Art's neighbour

Children will enjoy learning about the world right along with Teddy. Adults will marvel at Teddy's curiosity and world knowledge. And Teddy's musings will have both children and adults looking at their family pets and wondering what deep thoughts might be going on behind their sweet, adoring faces.

—Kelly Pulham
retired teacher
Brantford, Ontario, Canada

The stories, experiences, and communications in *Teddy's Dog Diary* are best summed up with these words: trust, intensity, honesty, and integrity.

—William Leonhardt
former high school principal
Brantford, Ontario, Canada

This is a great read to encourage us to involve dogs in our activities.

—Irene Leonhardt
retired teacher and real estate salesperson
Brantford, Ontario, Canada

Teddy's Dog Diary

Helen S. Pasanen

TEDDY'S DOG DIARY
Copyright © 2020 by Helen S. Pasanen
Photographs by A.A. Pasanen

All rights reserved. Neither this publication nor any part of this publication may be reproduced or transmitted in any form or by any means, electronic or mechanical, including photocopying, recording or any information storage and retrieval system, without permission in writing from the author.

This is a work of fiction. Names, characters, places and incidents either are the product of the author's imagination or are used fictitiously, and any resemblance to actual persons, living or dead, businesses, companies, events, or locales is entirely coincidental.

Printed in Canada

Print ISBN: 978-1-4866-1996-2
eBook ISBN: 978-1-4866-1997-9

Word Alive Press
119 De Baets Street, Winnipeg, MB R2J 3R9
www.wordalivepress.ca

Cataloguing in Publication may be obtained through Library and Archives Canada

Dedications and Thanksgivings

I dedicate this manuscript to Ann Farrugia, Teddy's caregiver, companion, and loyal friend. May all people, especially animal lovers, glean much inspiration and appreciation for God's created friends, dogs in particular.

Many thanksgivings to our heavenly Father for making the perspective from a dog's point of view so very enjoyable to write and experience.

A special thanksgiving to my husband, Arthur, who shared his contributions toward the writing of this book as well as being involved in the little treks Teddy had as he encountered "daily life" at 52 Dowden Avenue, Brantford, Ontario, Canada.

Contents

Introduction	xi
Day 1: Walks, Politics, and a Cat	1
Day 2: White Poodle Missing and Mouse Traps	5
Day 3: Country Living and Physics	7
Day 4: Bacon, Prayers, and Writing	11
Day 5: Different Communication and Sharing	13
Day 6: Fall Clean Up	18
Day 7: Skunks, Bones, and Stew	20
Day 8: Compost, Mice, and Glasses	23
Day 9: Curiosity, Wetlands, and a Visitation	25
Day 10: Power Failure and Vet Procedures	31
Day 11: Halloween, Research, Tricycle, and Garbage	34
Day 12: Mice, Rice, Thoughts, and Science	39
Day 13: Chip, Charlotte, Lab, and Daylight Savings Time Ends	42
Day 14: Sick, Inquiry, and an Offer	44
Day 15: Apartment, New TV, and Meat Burgers	46
Day 16: Ron, Carrots, Drunkards, and Water	51
Conclusion by Author Helen S. Pasanen	57

Introduction

Mum,

I'm writing this journal of my vacation with the Pasanens in letter format so that you can read it when you come home from England. It occurred to me that I could send you postcards every day, but because I'm long winded (talkative), that would mean sending at least a million altogether! By writing a long letter (day by day), I can give you all the juicy thoughts that come to me, and it won't cost me or the Pasanens any money for stamps. I'm just now wondering how much it would cost to buy a million stamps for a million postcards. My goodness, that amount of stamps times the price of one stamp (eighty-five cents, maybe) would be enough to decrease Canada Post's debt by almost a million dollars! I couldn't ask the Pasanens for that much money… could I, Mum?

You know, Mum, writing letters and reading books result in some interesting benefits for our bodies. Helen pointed out that when I express my joys, love, and frustrations in writing, my cholesterol count can go down. She says that a number of studies of children and young adults show that when a person writes letters that focus on meaningful, happy thoughts about a loved one, or thankfulness about something or someone, that person sleeps soundly and gets the rest needed for the next day. You can check Google for these tests.

I encourage all my readers to consider writing down their thoughts too. I don't mean texting. Texting has less value, and your spelling gets messed up. A texter who goes wild and spells improperly very seldom wins a spelling bee! When you write down your thoughts, whether they're happy, sound, or messed up, your stress level decreases and you become more self-aware. Some studies show that writing and reading enhance social connectedness. As you read *Teddy's Dog Diary*, you'll feel connected to me. I'm revealing stuff I never dreamed I would to anybody!

I know that as you read my account of things, you'll see a different side of dogs you never knew existed! Very few people stop to consider a lesson from a dog's perspective. I am an inquisitive dog, and I promise that this material will be inspiring, educational, and funny. I'm excited even now in my spirit, like I'm pregnant and about to give birth to a classic diary. Remember, this is a Cairn Terrier's perspective on daily living. I didn't have the privilege of going to school. I am self-taught. Mum, you were an excellent teacher about daily living. The activities and thoughts will be unedited and probably full of grammar errors, but ignore all that and concentrate on the heart issues I am relating. Be transported into my stories and see your empathy arise for the love and care of animals and people. See your own creativity and ability to process what you see and hear increase exponentially (at a high rate).

Grab a hot chocolate or tea and enjoy my commentary.

Much love,
Teddy Farrugia

Day One:
Walks, Politics, and a Cat

Dear Mum,

I recognized Helen and Art as soon as Liisa, your daughter-in-law, brought me into the house here on Dowden Avenue in Brantford—and I felt safe! I asked to go out and remembered the layout of the back yard, so with delight I claimed my territory for the coming two weeks. You do remember how dogs mark their territory? That procedure prevents turf wars, Mum. From time to time on the news, you hear about human gangs fighting each other over boundaries that have been crossed. Relationships, or unity in diversity, can get ugly as animal instincts rise up and a war begins. Don't worry, Mum, I'm not planning on joining a gang while I'm here. I have a purpose. I know I am loved and I belong to an awesome "grand-mum."

When Art takes me for a walk, and I know he will today, I go ballistic. I like to investigate where other dogs have marked their territory by sniffing every post, every tree, and every fire hydrant on the way. I do it every time, and I leave my mark too—if I have anything left in my bladder!

After Liisa had her cup of tea, she left for home. I hope by now, Mum, you have your curlers out of your hair, because you're going to be driven to that huge airport in Toronto by Liisa and your son.

I headed out again and noticed someone approaching the chain link fence. I made a beeline for the fence and barked a lot. Helen restrained me and told me to stop. It was a pretty woman who'd stopped to say a few words to me; she was friendly, so I shouldn't have barked at her! Helen told her that she and Art were babysitting me for two weeks, to which she replied, "God bless you for doing that!"

watch the baseball game: the Washington Nationals versus the Houston Astros. Helen usually cheers for the underdog, so with two great teams playing, she's not sure who she'll cheer for in this World Series. The Raptors basketball team was also playing, but Helen and Art can't get the Sportsnet One channel, because it's not part of the program package they purchased. I slept through most of the first four innings, after which Helen and I went to bed.

I knew there were mice downstairs because I sniffed them out the first night I was here. The trap in the laundry room went off, and sure enough, there was another dead mouse! That's number sixteen. How are they getting into the house? My friends don't know! The mice are mainly in the garage and in the attic, or so I've been told, but the odd one squeezes through a small opening into the laundry room, where there are two traps. Helen told me that the field mice across the road lost their field homes when the housing contractors built new homes for humans. The mice had no say in the matter and decided to harass Dowden residents. Helen and Art also have these high frequency sound devices, which I don't hear, but the mice apparently hate the noise and eventually leave the premises. It's best they go—their droppings are poisonous to humans. Mice must have better hearing than I do. Maybe I should get Helen to do some research on the different animals and how well they hear and see. That's fascinating, don't you think?

Day Two:
White Poodle Missing and Mouse Traps

I GOT UP WITH HELEN AROUND 6:15 A.M. IT RAINED DURING THE NIGHT BUT had stopped for now. I went out and felt free to roam the back yard. I looked for the cat but didn't see it. Perhaps that big broom Helen had in her hand the other night scared the daylights out of it! Who knows? I came back into the house, and as I munched on breakfast, Helen went back to bed. I followed after her, as she'd left the crate door open for me. At 9:30 a.m., Helen was back up and led me to the sliding door, but I didn't want to go out, as it was pouring rain. She seemed to understand that I didn't want to go out in that downpour! She seems content knowing that I will let her know when I really have to go to the bathroom!

It has turned out to be a lazy day with all the rain, so we became loafers for most of the morning. Art didn't get up until 10:00 a.m. Can you believe it? The rain stopped in the early afternoon, and I jumped for glee as Art got the leash and we headed out for our walk. He always stops to get the mail at the Canada Post boxes, but today there was no mail for them. That's how it goes sometimes, eh, Mum?

A neighbour lady Art had never talked to before stopped with her *toy* dog to ask Art a question. The toy dog totally ignored me. *Gads!* Does he have a rejection problem? Anyway, the lady told Art that her dog wasn't very social with other dogs and asked if he'd seen a white poodle on the loose. He had not. Someone has lost a dog. I know you would feel sorry for a lost dog, eh, Mum?

After dinner, Art went to a Life Group meeting in a nearby home. The group consists of people who discuss what they learned from the previous Sunday's sermon in church. Helen and I started downstairs to vote in the advance polls before leaving on your vacation, Mum? I'm underage, so I can't vote. Would they really allow a Canadian-born canine to vote? Anyway, I got bored with the political jargon and fell asleep on their red sofa.

About 8:30 p.m. or so, I had to go pee and told them politely. Art took me upstairs and let me out. I spotted a cat on the grass at the side of the stairs. It was dark-coloured and seemed sleepy, so I just walked on by and did my thing. The cat didn't move as Art approached it. Art was concerned about the look in its eyes as it intently watched me, so he chased it under the raspberry bushes. I decided not to bark or chase after it as I went up the stairs to the deck. It seems strange, Mum, that I haven't seen a cat that close-up before here on Dowden Avenue. I decided to take Art's spot on the blue sofa when I came in. It had a blanket on it and was so soft to sleep on. Art didn't mind. He came and sat beside me.

Helen turned the TV channel to the hockey game. It went into overtime. A stupid Leafs player took a stupid penalty and allowed a stupid penalty shot for the other team. The player who took the shot scored, and the Leaf team lost *again*! The Leafs are on a losing streak. Helen was getting bored with all the talk about politics and headed upstairs. I followed her, as I thought it was high time she went to bed.

Helen decided to follow me outside for my nightly you-know-what. I spotted the cat again in the raspberry bushes. I growled this time, and the cat hissed at me. I didn't like it when Helen pointed the corn broom at me. She didn't want us to fight and start a turf war. I gave in, did my job, and that was that. Helen went outside again without me, as she thought the cat was injured, but she couldn't find it. She said that usually the cats run for their lives when she opens the sliding door to the deck! They are wild cats—not domesticated. She told me about a neighbour who walks her dog for an hour every day. Mum ... a *whole hour* ... did you hear that? This lady also told Helen that she took in a stray cat. Before long, that cat had seven baby kittens. *Wow!* Can you imagine the fun I would have chasing them? Anyway, Mum, Helen did not want that kind of scenario duplicated here!

Then she continued on her walk. I wanted back into the house, because I remembered that Art was going to take me for a walk. In the back of my mind, I wondered how God was going to bless this couple who had opened their door of hospitality to me. Maybe I'm about to learn, eh, Mum?

I was patient. A fellow from a window company came to do some repair work on the kitchen window just as Art and I were to leave. He talked a lot, and as it turned out, he had been here before. He was a dark, handsome man with long braided hair falling back onto his shoulders in ringlets. You don't see that very often, do you? Finally, he left, and Art and I went out. Yes, Art had the poo bag too! I had to go before Art even reached the mailbox. You do know that it's important to pick up my litter, right, Mum? Because Art and Helen live on a corner lot, they're always picking up some dog poo, because some dog owners are inconsiderate and don't take responsibility for what comes naturally to us canines.

I manoeuvre pretty well up and down the stairs. Did you know that David, their son-in-law, put strips on the stairs leading to the back yard? I have no problem, Mum, because my paws can grip those strips, as they're like sandpaper. And up those stairs I fly!

Art decided to go somewhere with the truck, so I patiently waited for him to come home. I wondered if he would be getting me something. When he finally got home, I could smell the wonderful aroma of grilled chicken wrap ... I think! When they sat down to eat, I did too—right beside Helen. She is like you, Mum. She gives me treats after I've been outside, and when she eats, she remembers that I am waiting for *something good*. She saved me two small pieces of chicken—yes, they were good. I wondered if they do take-out a lot. I'll be in my glory if they do.

Helen asked me a funny question tonight: "Are you familiar with *politics*?" I didn't know what to say! Then they all headed downstairs to the rec room. Boy, when I got down there could I smell the mice! I sniffed everywhere but couldn't find them. I *know* they were there ... or had been down there. Anyway, I sure learned about *politics*. That's all they watched on TV!

Canada's Prime Minister was being chosen by the voters, and the results were being broadcast. Voting is a democratic privilege. Did you

Day Three: Country Living and Physics

AT 6:20 A.M. I GOT UP WITH HELEN, BUT I KNEW SOMETHING WAS DIFFERENT. She didn't sleep in very long after I had breakfast. She showered and then took the sheets off a bed and put them into a hamper. She puttered here and there and munched her breakfast as she went about working. Yes, I knew it—at 12:30 p.m., she put on her winter coat and went outside. I learned later that Liisa had picked her up for her specialist's appointment. She saw a hematologist—a blood specialist. She has a serious problem with her leg.

After Art finished his shower, he took me out for a walk. Helen came home an hour and a half later, and boy, was I glad to see her! I wagged my tail and barked excitedly. She's a special lady, just like you, Mum! I'm not sure if I should call her a lady. She wears these old patched jeans in the garden and in the house. Art also has jeans that are held up with stretchy dark-blue braces! Mum, they are not fashion-conscious people. They told me that they spent thirty-four years in the country living among the coyotes, wolves, lynx, deer, skunks, racoons, and other animals. They have the hearts of farmers. That's hard to believe, because Art was a nuclear physicist for many years working at Atomic Energy of Canada. What is the connection between agriculture and physics? I haven't got a clue. Do you, Mum?

On the other hand, there has to be a connection, as Art is always telling Helen how science or physics has proven some events in the Bible to be true. Helen talks about the intricate design of everything in nature as having a purpose. For example, the patterns of seeds in sunflowers or honeycombs made by bees are used in modern engineering. This technology is far beyond my understanding, but you can learn this stuff on the Science TV channel that Helen and Art watch. Everything on this earth is connected somehow and connected to its Creator in more ways than one.

Did you know that the airplane in which you flew to England was designed by someone who studied the physical structures of flying birds and insects? A God-inspired idea came to them, and the question came to me too: Why not put to use the little bird designs into one giant, huge bird to carry passengers from one continent to another? It obviously worked. You made it to England on the wings of a big bird! Don't confuse that with the yellow Big Bird from the TV show *Sesame Street*, because he can only hold one person at a time! Here I go again… I'm getting sidetracked. The main thing is that Helen always remembers to give me a treat after I do my duty outside! Art? Well, he usually forgets, but that's okay—I just go to Helen, and she knows what I'm asking for! Could it be that Art's thinking about physics instead of giving me a treat? Helen says that he fits the category of an absent-minded professor—and has since day one of their marriage back in 1962!

A fellow who parks his Edge SUV on Conklin in front of the kitchen window said hi to Art when he was out with me. He also said that I was a good-looking dog! How's that, Mum? I'm a smart-looking Cairn Terrier. The man also told Art that he wouldn't mind caring for me if Art needed a babysitter! Mum, I've got *star power* down here at Dowden.

Art's neighbour, Ron, likes to have his garage door open. On nice days, he sits in the garage, and sometimes people and their dogs visit with him. After I barked, he came to the fence line and talked with Art. Guess what, Mum? He had a treat for me. It was so delicious. Maybe I'll ask Helen if I could go out more often when I see the garage door being opened! Ron informed Art that they were getting a five-year-old dog in November or December. So the next time I come here, I'll get to meet her. Her name is Paula.

Their previous dog died of old age in the owner's arms. I've often wondered where dogs go when their life on earth is done. Helen says she has found several verses in the Holy Bible indicating that there are animals in heaven. I'm an animal … right, Mum? What are the qualifications to get to heaven, Mum?

Art left after dinner to run errands. When he came home at 9:30 p.m., I learned he had gone over to my brother's place. Your son and wife left early to go for dinner in Toronto. They were meeting up with a friend, Vikram, from Oxford University days—a doctor who was being presented with a special award for his research on global mental health. My brother Chip and friend Charlotte needed to be fed and let out, so Art was willing to go visit them. Isn't that nice? My friends are always willing to give a helping hand.

Day Four: Bacon, Prayers, and Writing

HELEN SLEPT IN THIS MORNING, AND SO DID I. WATCHING BASEBALL ON TV makes me tired. There had been some rain showers earlier, but by the time I got up, the rain had stopped. The wind was cold this morning, and I was hoping you had packed my winter coat, as next week is to turn even colder. Those weather people don't always get it right. They haven't perfected weather outcomes yet. Can anyone predict which way the wind will turn? Your guess is as good as mine!

Helen cooked up some millet porridge and stuffed raisins and cinnamon into it. That porridge did not appeal to me; however, when I was in the living room while Helen was trying to take pictures of me with her camera, a sweet aroma started coming from the kitchen. I recognized it as bacon and couldn't wait to see it cooked up. I was so disappointed when Art took his bacon slices and millet and sat down without giving me any. I knew who to pester and headed straight to Helen. I could see her four slices on her plate, and my mouth began to water. The smell was out of this world. I started to beg for some but was told to stop and wait until she had finished her breakfast. Mum, it smelled so good, I just had to say something. Helen doesn't like fat, so she trimmed it off. Pure bacon was coming my way, with no hormones, preservatives, antibiotics, or artificial ingredients. Pure enjoyment once I got chewing at it. I wondered how often they cooked bacon. She must have been reading my mind, because she said that it had been a long time since they'd last had bacon for breakfast. Oh well, every time I go outside, I'll try to get Ron's attention. I'm sure he'll understand my thoughts in my communicative barking: *Ron, are you listening? I'll have another one of your treats, please!*

After dinner, Helen and Art spent over an hour worshipping God in song, meaning that they followed the singing on a CD and then prayed for everybody under the sun. Mum, I've given a lot of thought to this prayer stuff. Instead of screaming and yelling at people, or fighting over turf and territories, why not love people through praying, or even saying the Lord's Prayer over them? That way, you allow God into your daily life. Now that is a profound statement coming from your beloved Teddy! I sat and listened to Art, who's usually stretched out on the sofa. Tonight he showed me grace and allowed me to be right beside him. I love that aspect of him. Helen is usually fully stretched out in her recliner.

I noticed that Helen often goes to the laptop computer on a small table in the living room. She doesn't sit too long, but tonight she just kept pressing down on the keys on the keyboard. She would sit and then stand. It seemed to go on forever, and finally Art and I went to bed. I heard her come to bed after midnight. Of course, I was curious about what she was writing. Perhaps, Mum, you're going to get another write-up about *me* and what I've been up to while you've been viewing the ocean in England. It feels like I'm going to birth a book or a puppy. I know I can't do that physically, but maybe prophetically. Maybe this time around I'll be gracing the cover of a doggie book that children will be eager to read. You never know with Helen. I wondered about her photo shoot with me the other day. What was that all about? Anything is possible in this particular household.

Day Five: Different Communication and Sharing

Sleepy Helen didn't get up too early this morning, although she let me out around 8:00 a.m. and fed me. When she finally did roll out of bed, she and Art talked for a long time. Some of their words aren't in my vocabulary, so my understanding of their conversation was disjointed. Do you know what I mean, Mum? I figured out they needed groceries, and the tires on the truck had to be torqued because the snow tires replaced the summer tires on their truck last week. I think that means the bolts holding the tires in place had to be tightened so that they wouldn't release and fall off while they were driving. That makes sense to me. Have you got your winter tires on yet, Mum?

Art also talked about ink. Helen is probably using the printer more often as she writes, and the printer is getting low on ink. With all that talk about doing things, I wondered if I'd miss my walk today with the busy boy, Art. Those walks are important to me, Mum. The smells along the sidewalks are really interesting. They're quite different from the ones you and I smell in our area of town.

Helen says the deciduous trees' leaves are beautiful. Orange, red, and yellow colours are all over this area. Am I colour blind, Mum? Dogs don't always see the same as humans, but our sense of smell is far greater than yours. I can smell a rat a mile away. I also know when a person isn't dog-friendly. I think God has placed within us a real sensitivity to dangerous situations. We just know automatically when something isn't right. I am literally tuned in to certain vibrations that you don't feel or see. Perhaps I'm moving in the supernatural realm, Mum. Anyway, it's exciting to be alive and tuned in to the created universe.

Before I get off this topic, did you know that trees communicate with each other? Helen showed me a book about the hidden life of trees. They can feel, smell, and talk. Did you know that, Mum? They share their needs and provide help for each other. This is proven by science. I am not kidding! Trees can distinguish if the tree growing beside them is the same kind as them! That's done through the root systems. It's neat how they form a sense of community, eh?

Forest specialists, called ecologists, are now able to see the amazing relationships within a forest through the communication system of sounds, electrical impulses, and chemicals. Trees can listen, just like I do when you speak to me. Trees can also respond. No wonder some people hug trees! Helen talks to trees and her flowers. She says it's important to bless not only her children but whatever she has been given to look after. I think Helen is one of those people who understands trees, as she saves every seedling that germinates on their property. She wants to protect them. I believe seeds tell each other that this property on Dowden Avenue at the corner of Conklin is the *best* place to put down roots. They're most likely to survive with a caregiver present. For listening to all this tree jargon, Helen rewarded me with my first Dentastix. You know I'm a good listener, don't you?

I knew there was something going on today, because Helen and Art were talking a lot this morning. My walk outside with Art was cut short, and he took off in their truck to go somewhere. No sooner had he come home than Helen went grocery shopping. She was back in under an hour.

After dinner, Art was kept busy getting brochures, cards, and books ready for a Gideon presentation at a men's breakfast tomorrow morning. The new Gideon for Brantford, Warren, was the main speaker, but Art had all the supplies needed for the display table. Have you heard of the Gideons International in Canada/Share Word Global? Helen told me that people who are called Gideons are Christians who are passionate about sharing the Christmas Good News of Jesus Christ's birth and the Easter story of Christ's death and resurrection. They volunteer to do that in many ways, including offering free copies of the Bible to children and adults. Knowing the truth about the Good News changed Art's life so much, he has worked as a Gideon for forty-seven years. The head office is in Guelph, Ontario; however, the men's breakfast is held in Paris. Mum, that is not the Paris across the English Channel from where you're vacationing. Paris is a twenty-five-minute car drive from West Brant.

Just as the sun was going down, I noticed that Ron had his garage door open. Usually he doesn't have the door open at this late hour. Then I wondered if Daylight Savings Time was drawing to a close for this year and if you were experiencing shorter hours of daylight in England. Art will be putting the clocks back one hour Saturday night. What the heck am I thinking about? It's timing I need to be worried about. I have to know the right time to be outside when Ron's garage door opens! I ran to the fence line, sat down, and waited for Ron. What on earth was he doing in that garage? I waited for what seemed like an eternity. When Art talked to me, Ron poked his head out and had something in his hand. I was sure hoping it was for me. It was! He handed me one of those delicious treats again. He knows how to make a dog's day better. Just think about it—I almost missed the treat because I was thinking about the time change! I wish we had a neighbour like Ron in our part of town. We're not quite human, but our owners are, and we do listen and communicate with people.

Before settling down to watch some TV, I had to go out again. I had drunk a lot of water. Art stayed on the deck while I made my way to the cedar trees. I sat down to look down the sidewalk. I thought I saw something move. I did. Someone was coming toward us, but what was that thing beside the person? Art kept asking, "What are you doing, Teddy?" Couldn't he see that I was standing—I mean, sitting—on guard? Finally, I saw a lady walking this tiny white dog. It was a lot smaller than me. I didn't move a whisker, but my eyes were riveted on the dog. When the pup spotted me, he barked. I barked right back at him. The barking startled the lady, and she quickly went past me without saying a word. I meant no harm. I was standing on guard for my friends.

Helen and I watched the Raptors basketball game. They lost to the Celtics. The Houston Astros are playing tonight but are trailing by two games in the World Series. Helen has started to cheer them on. We didn't watch the game too long but headed upstairs, because Art was setting his alarm clocks to 6:00 a.m. I'm sure we'll hear those alarms go off. Usually both Helen and Art are sound asleep at that hour. How do I know? Remember, Mum, I'm watching over them just like I watch over you when you're home. That's a dog's way of giving thanks for taking such good care of me each day of my life! I'm having fun here and hope you are too on your holiday, but I do miss you a lot at times.

Day Six:
Fall Clean Up

BOTH ALARMS WENT OFF AT 6:00 A.M. ART WAS UP IN TIME TO BE ON THE ROAD by 7:00 to go to the men's breakfast. *What might they be serving?* I asked myself. As I went outside, I realized it had been a cold night. There was frost on the grass and on the truck windows. The water in the bird bath was frozen solid. I guess it will be dismantled and put into the garage for the winter. Everything seems to go into the garage, or so it seems to me. I hope it doesn't snow before you come home, Mum. I hate the salty mixture in between my toes when I walk the sidewalks. You know the importance of washing that stuff off; otherwise, I could get an infection between some of my toes.

Art came home before 11:00 a.m. As he shared with Helen, I heard all about the meeting. It sounded really interesting. According to Art, the new Gideon made a wonderful presentation. After a cup of tea, Art wanted to take down the seven remaining rain barrels that catch rain water off the roof. *Is he going to take me for a walk? Surely, he won't forget that!* I thought. Before I knew what was happening, he had the leash in his hand and was taking me outside. There was no mail service today, because it was Saturday. There was no one else walking dogs today. How boring is that? Oh well, the exercise is good for me.

When we arrived back home, Art quickly went to take down the rain barrels (four catch barrels and three spares). The downspouts had to be adjusted too. Helen told me that the rain water comes in handy in times of drought. Last summer was hot and dry, and three times the barrels emptied. They had to rely on town water to keep the veggies and flowers from getting dehydrated. It would be nice if more people thought about conserving town water, eh, Mum?

While Art was labouring outside, Helen did some housework. Another day for laundry. By the way, she washed my two blankets last time, as I got them a little muddy. It took Art the better part of the afternoon to finish his cleanup. A batch of carrots still needs to be dug up. How do I know that? I went out several times to see how Art was doing. One time when I was checking things out, a cyclist went by really fast on Conklin. I barked as if I was out of my mind. Helen says that a club meets here in Brantford, and often she'll see seven or eight cyclists racing down the street. Perhaps they're in training for a race coming up soon. I noticed that Art didn't have time to dig up the carrots.

After dinner, they took showers and did the laundry. I figured that I would need a bath soon, as I mess around in empty gardens. They clean my feet when I come in, but that's not a real bath. Can I trust Helen to give me a bath, Mum? I guess you didn't pack my dog shampoo. She may have baby shampoo, which I hear is okay for dogs. I'll wait and see what develops.

Day Seven:
Skunks, Bones, and Stew

THIS WEEK HAS FLOWN BY. I'VE BEEN HERE SEVEN DAYS ALREADY. HELEN LET me out around 6:00 a.m. It had rained all night, but when she opened the sliding door, I was glad to see that the rain had stopped. When I came inside, she gave me my medicine mixed in with my food. I didn't finish the breakfast then but joined Helen for more shut-eye. Art was dressed by 9:00 a.m. and out the door by 10:00. Before he left, he let me out to explore the sounds and sights of the back yard.

I picked up a new scent near Helen's herb garden. Perhaps a skunk jumped the fence. Wendy, Helen and Art's neighbour, told them that she often sees skunks at 5:00 a.m. They love to ruin her lawns by digging up the grubs under the grass. I'm not sure what they look like, but they are food for the skunks. The skunks certainly exasperate Wendy, who wants them to go elsewhere, bringing the ordeal to an end. I laughed when Helen said that Wendy likes to take out her hose and spray the skunks with water. That power-hosing would get me running too. Incidentally, that hosing isn't as bad as what the protestors in Hong Kong are experiencing! I would call that "pressure to boot" over there in China, because the pressure-hosing is so strong, it could kill you! I don't think Wendy would want that for the skunks. She just wants them to keep moving down Dowden Avenue!

This morning Helen wasn't too talkative but instead concentrated on her writing. She kept going back and forth to the computer. To me, it seemed like exercise! At noon she disappeared into the kitchen, and I followed her there. Do you know, Mum, that all day yesterday I smelled chicken? Helen was boiling chicken bones with vegetables all day long.

That smell was torture for my nostrils. Can you imagine smelling chicken all day? The bones and veggies were thrown out, except for a few veggies that Art is going to put into his smoothie tomorrow. You should see what Art puts into those smoothies—everything except the kitchen sink. According to Helen, his nutritionist gave him all kinds of ideas for smoothies that would give him strength.

Helen had saved the chicken broth from those cooked bones and now began reheating it. Every now and then she would add a vegetable or two to the broth. I watched intently, because that chicken smell permeated the whole house. Then she did something really odd. Instead of using the cooked chicken in the fridge, she took out two large lamb chops. She browned them and then simmered them for quite a while. Gads, now I have two aromas to contend with! It mixed up my senses. She told me the chicken was for the next serving of stew, probably on Tuesday. Lamb is about to become reality, as she had planned on serving it and the stew for lunch when Art got home. She told me that they don't have lamb very often, so that means I won't get a taste of lamb again before you come home.

I was glad to see Art come through the front door. I barked with glee, because it was time for my walk. Walking has become my favourite time of day, next to begging for food. No one else was out walking today because it was raining. I thought of the rain gauge and wondered if the rainfall had reached forty millimetres as the weather man predicted. Weather-wise it has been a gloomy day. On our walk I counted two Canada Post mailbox depots on our route. When I came to Art's box, I slowed down. Art kept walking. *Did he forget his key?* I wondered. He informed me that it was Sunday and there was no mail delivery. Mum, he has to remind me, because I can't tell if it's a weekday or the weekend! It's not on my calendar. Do you think you could teach me the difference, or is it not important in a dog's life?

When Helen and Art sat down to have lunch, I sat right beside my friend Helen. Have I ever tasted lamb before, Mum? I don't recall the scent, but today's lamb scent was mixed in with that chicken broth smell that Helen used in the stew. She gave me five small pieces, the size of those tiny treats you left for me. I don't know that I would call lamb my favourite treat here, but I ate every morsel I was given. She's spoiling me, eh, Mum? I'll come home and start communicative barking, and you won't know that I'm asking for lamb! Keep it in mind, as I have cravings too. Ha ha!

I'll let you in on a secret, Mum. Every time Art goes on errands in the truck, he brings back two large green teas from McDonald's. My friends are playing the McDonald's Monopoly game. They've won at least fourteen food items, but they don't eat cheeseburgers and fries. They give the winning stickers to two boys in the area. I wonder if they have a dog?

Day Eight:
Compost, Mice, and Glasses

WHEN ART TOOK THE COMPOST PAIL OUTSIDE TO THE BIN, I WENT WITH HIM. Mum, where is the compost heap in our yard? Helen and Art save all the veggie and fruit peels and even small leftovers. Art places these in one of two bins. From time to time, he puts a compost activator, which he purchased from a hardware store or nusery, into the mix. In a few months' time, soil forms, which can go into their veggie gardens. Helen cautioned me by saying that we shouldn't put any meat products into the compost. We don't want coyotes on our doorstep begging for food!

Everything was wet because of the rain we had yesterday. Art checked the rain gauge, and sure enough, there was almost forty millimetres of rain in it. The weatherman was pretty accurate this time.

Art checked the many mouse traps and announced that he'd caught another mouse. He added that it was probably the final one. That particular mouse was really sneaky. The amount of peanut butter he consumed was outrageous. However, in his greed he made one fatal mistake. *Bang!* The trap went off and got him. Eighteen mice are now out of this house and gone to who- knows-where. What a terrible thought went through my mind. What if God lets those mice into the animal heaven, and one curls up on my head and falls asleep there? Holy cow, I'd better have a talk with God … don't you think, Mum?

Art went for an appointment with an eye specialist. His artificial lens needs to be cleaned off. He may need new glasses after that small surgery. He'll have to wait for a call to find out when he'll have it done. He's noticed that his eyesight, particularly when reading smaller print, hasn't been up to par. How come you never see dogs wearing glasses,

Mum? When I watch dog shows on TV, I occasionally see fancy dogs wearing sunglasses. Yes, sunglasses. How on earth do they stay on? Can you really train a dog to not move its head? Or do a nose dive to catch a fish? Or shake its head to remove the dust and grass gathered in it? In my case, it would be cedar twigs, as I love brushing up against those small trees. Humanity has its advantages, eh, Mum? In old age you get to see with glasses, and when you go out in the bright sun, you can put on sunglasses! Is that really fair?

It was pretty windy yesterday. Many of those coloured leaves on the local trees are miles away now. Art's lawn has a lot of leaves on it from the condo unit across Conklin Road. Some gusts of wind south of here reached ninety kilometres an hour. Helen said she wouldn't mind if every day was a colour-leaf day. She loves the Canadian fall season. The leaves are so pretty to look at. We should be so happy and thankful that we have four seasons in Canada. Each season has its beauty to display to us.

Around 5:30 p.m., I decided to go outside after being fed scraps of rainbow trout. I must say, that fish was okay. I went along the chain link fence and noticed a lady walking what appeared to be a black and white collie on the other side of Conklin. Art hadn't seen this dog before. I barked quite a few times to get his attention. He didn't change pace in his gait but walked disgustingly obediently beside his master. I tried to talk to the dog, but the only response was a disgusted look. Is that snobbery of the upper class, Mum? Should I be kind and say, "Well done, Collie, your obedience needs to be rewarded. Size isn't everything, after all." What a variety of dogs there are in this section of town! It has been such an education to see how they and their owners react to this vacationing canine—*me*! I hope people on the English coast are treating you well and are friendly. Like, who wouldn't stop and smile at you, Mum? You have the nicest smile this side of heaven!

Day Nine:
Curiosity, Wetlands, and a Visitation

WHEN I AWOKE THIS MORNING, HELEN TOLD ME THAT I HAD BARKED SEVERAL times in my sleep last night. She asked, "Who were you chasing, Teddy?" I don't remember, Mum. You dream too, don't you? Do you ever write your dreams down on paper, Mum? Helen says dreams speak to her, and sometimes she gets prayers answered through her dreams. No wonder she is called prophetic! I'm not really sure what that means. It sounds interesting and intriguing.

When Helen opened the slider door this morning, I was almost blown over by the blanket smell of skunk! The smell was really irritating. Helen wanted to make sure the skunk wasn't in her back yard, so she grabbed the big flashlight and scanned the yard. It was free of skunks. She was protecting me this time. I quickly did my job and scurried back into the house. Why do you think God gave these skunks such powerful, awful perfume to spray at us? I wish the smell was more like your perfume … Miss Dior, or whatever it's called!

Are you getting tired of all my questions yet? It seems I've become a more curious dog since coming here. This curiosity is in the atmosphere, I think. That's why all those mice got into trouble. They were curious to find out how the peanut butter tasted and what brand it was. *Pow!* And they were gone. I'm not so curious that I'd nestle up to a skunk! That would be gross. Poor Helen and Art would be pouring tomato juice or white vinegar all over me to get rid of that terrible perfume!

Two ladies, Barb and Debbie, came to visit Helen. I barked because I'd never met or smelled them before. Helen assured me they weren't from that organization that keeps changing its doctrine. They grabbed a coffee and one cookie each and headed into the living room to chat. I don't know if "chat" is the right word. Helen was going a mile a minute. She's never at a loss for conversation.

Soon Art put me on my leash, and off we went. He decided to take me to the two ponds at the end of Bradley Street. The park is called D'Aubigny Creek Wetlands. It has recently been excavated. Some workers from the City of Brantford also paved the walk. It's been transformed into an environmental paradise. In my joy at experiencing this wonderful place, I went through some small bushes. Mum, neither I nor Art saw this coming. My tail and back were filled with burrs! I was upset, but Art said he'd help me remove them all, even if my grooming style changed. I vaguely recall this park from my last visit here. It was so different then—messy and with weeds seven times taller than me. Mum, why is it important to have burrs hidden in the natural landscape of nature? Why didn't those crew members remove them? How do the skunks get rid of those burrs? They can hardly see. They are one species that could use glasses, Mum.

After the special grooming session (getting rid of the awful burrs), Art joined the ladies in conversation. He talks a lot more than I remembered. Before long, they were talking about Chernobyl, where some nuclear accident occurred years ago. Do you think that these ladies would be interested in that topic? I was surprised when I saw that they were. Can you believe that? I didn't know that Art was responsible for figuring out why the accident occurred. He used physics to do that. He and his team of physicists from Canada uncovered a flaw in the design of the reactor safety system that contributed to the severity of the accident rather than preventing it, as it was supposed to. Besides that, the Russians had violated six safety rules in an attempt to complete a testing program ordered by the government. Why on earth would they think it was okay to go beyond the boundaries of safety? People's lives were at stake. The Russians wouldn't admit any wrongdoing until months later.

I'm learning that this Art I've come to know has played a great part in Canadian nuclear history! Helen tells me that Art has proven some top scientists (top dogs in the industry, Mum) to be wrong in their physics calculations. He doesn't mind that others got credit for work he did, either. As long as God knows, that's all that matters to him. Art believes his wisdom comes from God. This couple babysitting me is no ordinary couple, Mum. How did you get to know them?

It was time for the ladies to leave. They wanted to pray for Helen. *Well, this is interesting*, I thought. They placed hands on her and started to pray in some language I didn't know. I was curious, so I moved into a position between the two ladies who were on either side of Helen. Soon I joined in and agreed with what they prayed. I saw Helen's hand and gave it a tender lick before I sat down. Art was watching me all this time. Did I do right, Mum? I've never entered into prayer before, and it felt good to be part of that experience. Do you know of any other dogs doing what I just did?

After the ladies left, Art ran some more errands. Yes, he came home with another two green teas from McDonalds. This time the stickers were duplicates and couldn't be used on the Monopoly gameboard. Art thought it best to stop going for those green teas! He's probably right.

While Art was away, I watched Helen prepare supper. You won't believe what she added to the turkey meatloaf. Besides the usual herbs that were grown in her own back yard, she rolled some rice cereal with a rolling pin! She added ground flax and chia seed instead of eggs. Then she added finely chopped zucchini and kale. My mouth did not salivate at that! Why is she spoiling my meat platter? She read my thoughts again, Mum. She told me that these two vegetables are often used in meat dishes in Italy and Greece. She's not even Italian or Greek! Her parents are from Finland, as are Art's. You didn't taste the likes of these when you were in Greece, did you, Mum?

She added real turnip—not rutabaga—into the same pan as the meatloaf. Then she threw in some parsnips and whole carrots that she grew in the garden at the back of her deck. This was not looking good at all. Beside the pan in the oven she placed four small yams. Then Helen and I retired to wait in the living room.

I fell asleep and dreamed that I didn't have to eat those veggies at my treat time! When dinner was served finally, I sat near Helen. She decided to separate the veggies from the turkey meat. She was careful not to leave onions on the meat, because she was concerned that I'd get an upset stomach. Some veggies just don't agree with dogs. Now how considerate was that? Those veggies were eliminated! It did smell as if something had burned in the oven. Two yams had started to leak, and the juices oozed to the oven floor. Helen forgot to put a bit of foil under those yams. She didn't mind, though, because she has stumbled onto a new thing, which is actually quite an old thing—a recipe to clean up burnt blobs in the oven. Want to know the secret? She makes a paste with baking soda and water and places it over the burned areas. Every now and then, she adds a few drops of water into it and leaves the whole thing overnight in the oven. Around mid-morning the next day, when she starts moving around doing chores, she wets the burned areas with a little water again. The dirt, which has now soaked into the baking soda, easily lifts off, and miraculously the oven is spotlessly clean after rinsing and drying the area! Occasionally she has to use a wooden flipper to rub off the more baked-on blobs. Mum, is that an old English trick for cleaning ovens?

While Art went to another Life Group meeting, Helen started writing again. I wondered if she knew there was a Leafs hockey game and a World Series baseball game on tonight. By the way, is the term "eh" strictly a Canadian slang word, or does it come from England? It's spoken all the time here. Helen loves that term. She finally came down with me to watch TV. We were disappointed that the Nationals won the game and that the final game is tomorrow. Helen flipped the channel to the Toronto Maple Leafs game. That Leafs' player who signed a multi-million-dollar contract recently took a stupid penalty in the overtime period, and the Leafs lost again! Why is he being paid so much money to lose games? Explain this rationale to me please, Mum. It's this kind of nonsense that makes me sleep through most of the games! I know our hometown-grown, former hockey player Wayne Gretzky—the Great One, as he was called—would never flounder away the team owners' money like that, or the money received from ticket sales. He won games. Maybe I shouldn't call him the "Great One," because that's idol worship, and I could get in trouble, spiritually speaking. Only God Almighty can be called the Great One, for He is greatly to be praised.

Day Ten:
Power Failure and Vet Procedures

THE FORECAST WAS FOR SHOWERS TODAY WITH POSSIBLE SUNNY BREAKS IN THE afternoon. It rained most of the day. It was still dark when I was let out, and I noticed the puddles on the road because the street lights were still on. By 1:00 p.m., the time when I go out for my walk, it was still raining. Art didn't mind, because he has a waterproof jacket, although Helen thinks differently. The leash went on and I trotted out with Art. I didn't have a waterproof jacket, so by the time I got home, I was soaked through and through. Helen had a green towel ready for me, and Art had the chore of drying me off. It was like having a bath, Mum.

I forgot to tell you that around 9:30 a.m. the electricity went off. It came back on briefly and then stayed off until just before 10:00 a.m. The power at the plaza across the road was off as well, as were the signal lights at Shellard Lane and Conklin Road. Helen was watching the traffic at that intersection, as she could see it from her recliner quite easily. She seemed to get upset when she noticed cars and trucks on Shellard just zooming through the intersection, while those on Conklin were very carefully coming to a stop before proceeding. Fortunately, no accident occurred and the lights came back on. Don't these people testing new vehicle drivers emphasize safety? When the signal lights are out and there is no one directing the traffic, the driver needs to slow to a crawl and stop before advancing ... right, Mum? Maybe some of those older drivers and teens need a refresher course ... or to stop driving altogether.

Art saw a fire-truck and an ambulance, and Helen saw a Brantford Power truck, go west on Shellard. Art concluded that maybe a careless driver had lost control and hit a hydro pole, disconnecting the power.

Helen thought it could be a fibre optic contractor slicing a powerline in the area. They're placing huge cables into the ground south of Shellard, and those contractors are notorious for cutting other companies' cables and underground wiring! Notice I said "notorious" and not "notornis," which is a rare, flightless New Zealand bird with a large bill and beautiful plumage. When I think about it, maybe those workers are flightless in their thinking! Anyway, they are notorious for cutting other companies' cables and underground wiring! Ask Helen about it—neighbours do talk about inconveniences. That's not gossip, is it? It's a way of letting friends know that they're not the only ones struggling with the inconveniences that others inject into community living. Maybe tomorrow there will be a brief notice in the local newspaper as to why the power shortage occurred.

If you were to ask Art about those fibre optic cables, he'd tell you something interesting about them. He told me that instead of digging an open trench in which to lay the cables, engineers designed a machine with the power to push steel pipes thirty metres through the ground in sections three metres long. It has the power to apply a force of one thousand kilograms to the pipes to push them even through rocky ground. The fibre optic cable is carried inside the pipes and left in the ground after the pipes are removed for reuse in the next thirty-metre section. Did you get that, Mum? It took me awhile before it sunk into my mind!

Isn't it neat how trained engineers and scientists can apply God-given laws of physics and mathematics to design amazing machines like this particular machine? I'd like to add to this technology by asking a question, Mum. Why didn't those educated people add a camera and a radar gun to the front of those steel pipes so they could detect a live powerline underground? Then the residents in the areas where they're working wouldn't have needless power outages! Maybe they should have asked for my opinion and Helen's on the design of those machines. We think alike in most cases—teamwork is what I like to call it.

Wasn't that fascinating, Mum? Art's curiosity led him to ask a bearded man who was operating one of the machines to explain how they worked when they were installing the cable in front of Art's house. I won't share all the problems Art and Helen had when the servicemen hooked up their computer and TV to the new system, but I will say that they had four different service people come four different times to do four different things to try to get their devices to work properly on this new Bell system! *That* says a lot, eh, Mum? Helen thinks those men were not trained adequately on the new system before attempting to hook it up. They were learning as they went along and guessing—to beat the band, so-to-speak. Can you imagine the frustration for the customers? Companies, lend your ears this way. Train your people before setting them out to do the work! Okay?

I remember from the last time I was here that there's an animal clinic across from Helen and Art's, but I'm not able to see any dogs or cats going in through the clinic's side door because Helen's "flower" table is full of aloe plants, African violets, a spider plant, and an orchid. The table sits in front of the window facing the clinic, and the flowers obscure my view. Do you recall me telling you, Mum, about an embarrassing act those two vet assistants perform with dogs at this clinic? They bring the dog out, and with scoops they catch either the dog's poo or urine! How humiliating is that? They need samples, but can they not do it inside so the whole world doesn't witness it? I never once saw them do that for a cat. Never! There is a favouritism issue at this clinic for sure.

Day Eleven:
Halloween, Research, Tricycle, and Garbage

HELLO, HALLOWEEN! RAIN, RAIN, GO AWAY, COME BACK ANOTHER DAY! MUM, they have cancelled Halloween activities in Montreal, Quebec because the system that has brought this heavy rain will batter the Montreal area with ninety to one hundred kilometre an hour winds! Can you see those small children, the trick or treaters, being tossed about and thrown down the streets of Montreal? Good call by the government officials in Quebec! No parties cancelled here that I know of, but it's still raining. Maybe I should steal some of those chocolate bars that will be left over. I know for sure we won't have very many knocking at our door tonight. Maybe I should throw my wish down the drain, Mum. Stealing is never right. It's one of God's Ten Commandments—don't steal. Yes, I also remembered that chocolate is not good for dogs. Some dogs have left this planet because they became so sick on chocolate.

I started thinking of an incident that happened before you left for England, Mum. I am ashamed of it now. You always tell everyone what a good boy I am because when food is on a low table, I don't touch it. Well, one day when you were having a lunch of crackers, cheese, and fruit down in the family room, the doorbell rang. You and I went upstairs to see who it was. It was Liisa. After saying hello, I decided to go back downstairs where your lunch was. I waited and waited for you to come downstairs, but you continued talking and laughing with Liisa. Anyway, I got tired of waiting, and my appetite came back full tilt. I took one cracker. Boy, it was good. Before I knew it, I had eaten all the crackers. Liisa couldn't stay, as she was dropping something off down the road. After she left, you came down to have your lunch. Boy oh boy, was I in big trouble, even though I didn't touch your cheese or fruit. I tried to explain that it must have been the medication you'd been giving me, because I wasn't eating. I hadn't been well, and I had lost two pounds, which worried you to no end. You had gotten the medication from the vet to ease my pain and help bring my appetite back. You see, it really wasn't my fault, Mum! Somehow you seemed to understand, and I promised not to do that again.

Before we had this heavier downpour, I was outside and came running up the deck stairs when I saw Ron's car pull into the driveway. I went down those stairs so fast, I almost slipped on my behind. I ran to the fence like a bullet. I barked to let Ron know I was there. I waited and waited and then heard the car door shut. I listened. Those were not Ron's footsteps. For crumbs' sake, they were his wife's! She proceeded to go into her house and never looked my way. At the thought of getting a treat I was now licking my chops for nothing. Do you think Ron forgot to tell Yvonne that he treats me to something very delicious? Maybe he does it behind her back and she doesn't have a clue that I was anticipating the treat! Mum, how can I relay this message to her? This has to do with community living. Any ideas come to mind?

Helen and Art had another worship and prayer time. Today they were more specific and prayed for Brantford, the trick or treaters, and even for my English Mum! Talking to God is so easy for them. It's like talking to you or me. It's like they know this person, God. Anyway, I am glad to be part of their lives.

Three days or so ago, on this very beautiful fall day here, I was enjoying being alive. I was near Helen's comfrey bush when I happened to look south on Conklin. My eyes bulged out of my head. There at the corner of Conklin and Dowden was the biggest tricycle I had ever seen in my life. It was humongous, and there was a man, not a child, sitting in it! I barked and barked to see it. The man steered it onto the road leading to the condos across the street. I thought to myself that there was no way I could handle that tricycle. I am too small. Helen also saw the tricycle, and when I came into the house, she had a sad story to tell about the man on the tricycle.

All his life this man had been an outdoors man and loved racing his bike across the land. He even went overseas to go to top competitions, like the Tour de France. One day he wanted to buy a better and faster bike. An American champion had recently designed a bike and was selling them all over the world. He purchased one. He took it for a fast testing. Sometime into the race, the handle bars collapsed and fell off, sending him flying into the air. He suffered many injuries and became a paraplegic that day. That means he has no use of his legs because of the spinal injury he suffered. The tricycle I had seen was specially made for him so that he could get out and exercise a little. He uses his hands to peddle. This is such a sad story, Mum. His wife, who is now eighty-three years old, told Helen the story one day as she was out walking alone. Many lawsuits are pending regarding this flawed bicycle. Sounds similar to the flaws in the Boeing 737's airplanes, eh, Mum? I wonder if dogs make as many mistakes as humans—I mean, serious mistakes.

Art took me for a wet walk. It has been raining most of the day. I got another bath, again with no shampoo. Helen has been scribbling a lot today, and I know tomorrow the computer "Word" system is going to record her thoughts that are on her scrap pages now.

Art briefly spoke with Ron and his wife, Yvonne. Art inquired about the dog they will soon be getting. Yvonne told him that the wait time is very similar to waiting for a real baby to arrive. They are both eager to get this dog. It is not a Cairn Terrier. There are so many breeds of dogs and lots of Heinz 57s. That means they are cross-breeds, as the father was a different breed from the mother.

Those trick or treaters will be here soon, and it is still pouring rain outside. It was a slow start with only twelve children coming for treats from 5:30 p.m. to 8:00 p.m. Helen was willing to hand out the treats plus a special children's book to them. Art had gone downstairs to watch TV and called me down to join him. He put up a small barrier at the bottom of the stairs so I couldn't run up the stairs to bark at the children. I was sitting beside him on the couch, and Art laid his left hand gently on the harness strap on my back. I knew this meant I was to "stay put" for a while.

Mum, do you know I was really obedient and did not say a word when those twelve children came to the door! After 8:00 p.m., Art took over handing out the treats, and Helen came downstairs to watch TV. I stayed with her, but I had the couch to myself as she lay on the recliner. Since she was not beside me, I decided it would be okay for me to put my front paws at the top of the couch so I could have a bird's eye view of the children coming in. It was like an alarm went off. Another eighteen children, mostly older boys, showed up. I saw a lot of different costumes, and some were scary. After 8:45 p.m. there was no more knocking. You would have been proud of me, Mum, because I still did not bark at them, even though I was alone on the couch!

I'm not sure how this "trick or treat" night came about. Helen did some research on the matter. She is always looking up facts. The mainstream faith groups would have nothing to do with this pagan festival that originated a long time ago until it weaved itself into them, with permission, because it became a cultural norm. In Canada, the idea of trick or treat apparently originated in a city in Alberta in the 1800s. Helen asked me these questions. Why are so many costumes so scary? Why do adults open a haunted house that scares the wits out of people? Fear to this day bothers some sensitive people who were frightened at Halloween when they were youngsters. What tricks are performed by the ones who do not get treats? What good are all those sugary treats? The sugar causes tooth decay and much more. Helen said a dentist in Halton Hills would buy candy that his patients had picked up at Halloween. He would give them so much money per pound or kilogram to save them from eating all that sugar that would cause tooth decay. He really cared for his patients, Mum.

A cult that started this event has celebrated Halloween for centuries. I didn't want to research them, but we should know about things like this. Why do people make Halloween a billion-dollar industry, worldwide? Have our minds been screwed or lied to? Where are the principles of truth we need to follow? I never thought about it that way until Helen said that I should do my research.

Speaking of stinking thinking, I have to tell you something about real garbage that I see every time I go for my walk. Over at the plaza, especially at the pizza take out, quite a few students from the local high school gather at noon and on breaks to eat, do drugs, or vape e-cigarettes. Some school kids don't respect the premises where they buy food. Crusts of pizzas and submarine buns are thrown all over the place. I see seagulls from Lake Erie dive bomb for crusts. The birds don't eat the Styrofoam or paper plates, so they are left there. How awful is this? Canada the beautiful at this plaza becomes a garbage dump, and students are responsible. Polluters have been around a long time, unfortunately, and this conduct makes for unsightly sights. What can be done for these people whose behaviour reveals an "I don't care attitude?" The majority of kids at that school are really decent. They have canvassed for the poor in the area and for other good causes. As Art says, "It only takes one bad apple to spoil the bushel!"

While it's still on my mind, I wish to report that the Nationals, who were the real underdogs, won the World Series. We rejoiced because it had been decades since they'd won such a championship. Good for them!

Day Twelve:
Mice, Rice, Thoughts, and Science

MUM, YOU WILL NOT BELIEVE WHAT I SAW THIS MORNING. AT 8:15 A.M., HELEN let me outside. There on the rooftops, on the grass, and on the deck flooring was that white stuff—*snow*. Those strong winds last night ushered in the zero temperatures and a lot of flurries. By 10:00 a.m., the snow had melted, as the temperature reached four degrees Celsius. Winter is coming early, which is why the mice sought shelter in Art's insulated garage so early. There were sunflower seeds in that garage to last for years for those mice until Art secured those seeds in a sealed container. Two more mice were caught three days ago, making that twenty altogether. Art is hopeful there are no more. He figures those sonic devices drove the mice to the garage level from the attic. With the sunflowers stashed away, the mice went after the bait in the traps. Zoom! They are all gone.

It's now near supper time and the sun is shining and blue skies are overhead. What a mood changer for me. Helen just whispered and said I shouldn't get my hopes up, as there is only one nice day ahead in the next five days! Where is all this rain coming from? It needs to be sent to California where hectares of land are burning. The situation needs lots of prayer. Very dry conditions and very high winds are factors in spreading the fires. Some Canadian hydro workers have gone to help restore power lines destroyed by the fires. That gesture is greatly appreciated by those American neighbours of ours.

Helen and Art enjoyed their dinner. They have a special liking for honey and garlic ribs. I was eating my regular kibbles when Helen started to prepare the ribs. *The heck with my food*, I said to myself, and I made a beeline to her feet. It smelled heavenly. I wasn't sure of the rice dish, though. She made it yesterday and added veggies to it. She puts veggies into every known dish she makes! She showed me the rice package and read out the four different kinds of rice. Mum, it is *wild rice* indeed. One is called whole grain Wehani rice. What on earth is that? The last one was called whole grain Black Japonica. Where do they grow japonicas? A company name appeared on the rice package: Velcro Industries. Do you think they added that Velcro material used as a fastener to keep the rice together? God forbid that is true.

I got thinking about the number *twelve*. Maybe I should call my unedited letter report to you "The Twelve Days of Christmas"—*not quite*. It's been like Christmas every day here. I would, however, miss writing over the next four days, as you don't get home until late Tuesday night. Let me chew on that thought for a while. I'm beginning to sound like Helen, eh, Mum? She chews on thoughts that come to her and then laughs away as streams of nonsense and ideas flood her brain. Does God ever give us thoughts? If you were to ask Helen, she would say, "You bet your bottom dollar He does!" You see, Mum, the saying goes, "Thoughts become my words; my words become my actions; my actions become my values; my values become my destiny." She says those statements are found in the Bible. Tap into a thought, Mum. Run with it. See where it will take us, Mum.

What is that noise I hear coming from outside? It's a lawn mower. My goodness, it's nearing 6:00 p.m. and it will soon be dark. It's Art. I begged Helen to let me out. I raced to see him mulching leaves on the median strip and his front lawn. Apparently, he read that this mulching is good for the grass as winter approaches. He knows best, I guess.

Helen really gets "high" reading the magazine they subscribe to called *Discover—Science for the Curious*. There are so many interesting articles in it. In the last issue they received there was one article that caught her attention. It's called "The Power of Cute." It may explain why people are attracted to me! Then I heard Helen say that there is a sentence that says that humans are still learning what "cute" does to human brains and behaviour. I know when I see a cute object or living thing, my brain activity heightens. I desire to nurture, protect, and care for it. Studies show that not all respond so positively. That explains why community doesn't always happen in the home, groups, churches, organizations, and other groups. The psychologists mentioned stuff in that article that is all Latin to me. From my own experience, I do know when someone is cute. I will socialize and befriend them, even though we're not related. Future brain scans detecting activity may unearth a lot of answers to questions humans have when encountering cute babies, cats, dogs, mice, and other creatures. But let us look at the simple, positive side. My cuteness always stimulates something good within you, Mum. Let us leave it at that and forget about all those speculations and possibilities researchers come up with, okay?

Day Thirteen:
Chip, Charlotte, Lab, and Daylight Savings Time Ends

Here it is Saturday, and it's raining again. The phone rang this morning, and it was Liisa. I overheard the conversation. She has invited us for tea! I get to see my brother, Chip, and Charlotte. Maybe, just maybe, they will drive me home.

I reminded Helen often about the tea. At first she didn't understand my different bark, but she caught on and assured me that she would not forget about going to my brother's place. After showers, laundry, and other small jobs, they put me in the back seat of the truck with Art right beside me. I could hardly wait to see Chip again.

He was so happy to see me. Charlotte? Well, she showed off with a new toy rag. Only once did she growl because she had possession of that toy. She thinks she is the Alpha dog in the house. Helen brought my dinner, but I was too excited to gobble it up in one sitting. You wouldn't believe how many times Chip and Charlotte wanted to eat my dinner! Peter had to guard it with all his might.

I really enjoyed running in the back yard with Chip, and those tiny treats they gave me made my day. Their stairs were slippery, so I asked them to carry me up. I didn't want to fall and hurt my back-end. I would jump onto their chesterfield and dream you drove up in your car. I went back to Helen and Art's a wee bit sad. I know the next three days will go by fast.

When Art took me for a walk, I had an interesting surprise. As we were walking by a driveway on Bradley Street, a big Golden Lab came out of the house quickly to meet me. The owner had opened the door to go somewhere and didn't realize his dog had spotted me and Art, and the dog zoomed by him before he could stop it. He sniffed me and then I sniffed him, and all was okay. He was a friendly type of dog. His owner ran out quickly and called him back and then apologized to Art. No harm was done and we carried on as usual.

Helen heard on the news tonight that England was getting pretty strong winds too. In fact, the ferry service across the English Channel was stopped for a bit. That storm was probably the remnants of the storm that closed down Halloween in Montreal, Quebec, Canada.

The clocks were changed before Helen and Art went to bed. We get to sleep in for an extra hour.

Day Fourteen:
Sick, Inquiry, and an Offer

I DIDN'T MEAN TO AWAKEN HELEN AT 7:00 A.M., BUT I HAD A SICK FEELING AND vomited at the edge of my crate. Helen didn't seem to mind. She scrubbed the area and my bed mat with soap and rinsed it well. Since the foam label was still on the bottom, she read it carefully. Because there's not to be strong heat or sparks near the bedding, she folded my bed mat over the bathroom towel railing. Every time the furnace went on, the warm air from the ducts blew onto the wet area. It was dry in no time at all.

I went out and really felt much better having given up stuff. Helen examined the vomit and said there was a full piece of a treat, still intact, that had been given to me before I went to bed. I had swallowed it whole without biting it. It wasn't a Dentastix. Helen decided to wash my other two towels, and they are now clean for when you come home.

Laura, the daughter of David, Helen and Art's son-in-law, brought over her two daughters, Erica and Charlotte, and we had lunch together. Helen wanted Erica's opinion about the record I am keeping. Helen wanted a perspective from a ten-year-old. She wanted to know if it was good reading, if there should be changes, and if she had any pointers about improving it. Helen got some good feedback, and we will make changes down the road, should this material be put into the form of a children's book. I think Helen will get some other feedback from older children too. Mum, I think what I experienced here is exciting and the whole world should know about my vacation. What do you think?

Our walk today featured another man. I noticed he was out smoking a cigarette by his open garage door, so I tried to pull Art up this fellow's driveway. Maybe he's another Ron waiting to give me a treat! Art told him about his neighbour, Ron, and to Art's face he said that all he had to give was a cigarette. I am not a smoker. Imagine giving me a cigarette in broad daylight. I wondered why he would even say what he said to Art. Anyway, we continued on our way, and I wasn't tempted to go up any more driveways except Art's.

Day Fifteen:
Apartment, New TV, and Meat Burgers

WELL, THE DAY BEGAN WITH A LITTLE RAIN, BUT AS IT PROGRESSED, THE RAIN came to a stop. Both Helen and Art were at the computer a lot this morning. I was beginning to wonder if Art was going to forget my walk. Then he stretched and headed to the front door. I wasn't far behind. He did not forget. The leash was put on me and out we went. Today was a weekday, so Art stopped for the mail, and so did I. Helen told me that an interesting development was occurring at the corner of Shellard and Conklin. An apartment building is being proposed at that corner, and the facts came in the mail in the form of a couple of pages. They are proposing a community garden also at that lot that now lies vacant. That is up their alley, so to speak. If Helen and Art live long enough, they can move into that apartment building. They are seriously considering downsizing. Do you know what that means, Mum? I would think it would take a few years to build that apartment building, eh, Mum?

Art has gone out again and is going to some tech shop. He wants a new TV, as the other one downstairs is old. He can't play his DVDs since the fibre optics cable came into this house. They found out that the system doesn't work on old TVs that have old DVD players. This time he's going to mount it in the living room, apparently for a number of reasons. There's already a TV mount screwed into one wall. It was hiding behind a picture all the while I was here! It's in an ideal position. Apparently, this store will send out a fellow who will hook up the new TV. That suits them just fine. I'm anxious to see if he goes ahead today and brings home a new TV. I'll wait and see.

While he was out, Helen was busy washing a bunch of carrots. They were dug up some time ago but never washed. Art believes in leaving them dirty. Helen, who does the cooking, prefers to handle washed carrots, like the ones you get in the store, Mum. She has mentioned digging up more carrots in the last garden beside the apple tree before the real cold weather comes. Art is thinking of covering those "still-in-the-ground carrots" with bags of leaves that he hopes to get from Peter and Liisa. That way the carrots are insulated against freezing temperatures, and the ground under them never freezes. Apparently, Art did this where they used to live. Helen believes she can get all those carrots cleaned up and put into her fridge or even into the garage for storage. Two schools of thought, eh, Mum? Which would you prefer if you had all those carrots to dig up?

I've been watching, almost on a regular schedule, through the glass door leading out to the deck. I can see from there when Ron comes home and opens the garage door. Just a few minutes ago there he was in front of an open garage door. I made sure he heard me as Helen allowed me outside. My voice has changed a few octaves since coming here, Mum. I can reach those high-pitch notes! He heard my melody and approached me. Yes, oh yes, in his hand was a treat for me. Oh, how I will miss these heavenly, celestial encounters with Ron when I go home. I shall dream of him often. He has been so kind to me. I wonder when their new dog is arriving. I just know she will be well taken care of.

Well, Art came home all excited! He said he struck a deal with this tech guy. The new TV will be delivered on Wednesday—the very morning I am headed home to you. At least that's what I have been told. Art took a photo of the TV mount before leaving and there are two vertical pieces missing, so the tech man gave Art another mount from the store, which they had used. It was sold for a very reasonable cost to Art. Perhaps next time I will get to watch it and see some of these DVDs they've been wanting to watch.

I saw a TV ad last night that got me questioning meat burgers. What is the difference between an Angus burger and just an ordinary hamburger? Are there cattle that are called Angus? Jersey cows are dairy milk producers, right, Mum? Are they ever used to make hamburgers in fast food restaurants? Helen took me to a page on Google to show me some cows. Gads, there were dozens and dozens of different breeds. Are you familiar with any of these: the Holstein-Friesian, the Hereford, the Brangus, the Highland, the Shorthorn, the Texas Longhorn, the Red Poll, or the Beefmaster? Just curious, Mum.

Day Sixteen:
Ron, Carrots, Drunkards, and Water

WELL, I HEARD THROUGH THE GRAPEVINE THAT YOU ARE COMING HOME LATE tonight. Hurrah! I slept in until 7:15 a.m. and was glad to get outside.

When I came inside, I noticed that Helen still had that rain gauge standing upright on the counter. She had put some white vinegar into it to soak and release all that dirt that had collected in it since the spring. Helen says that this same rain gauge was used on their country property in Erin, and never once did she have to use vinegar to remove the dirt. I, as she, wondered if the air pollution is worse down here. Mind you, it's nothing like the pollution in a city in India right now. Children have not had to go to school for three days. It has been like thick foggy days in London town, England, eh, Mum?

I was so happy to get a treat from Ron so early this morning. I was in seventh heaven. Maybe that will be my final one for this vacation. When I was still outside, a truck and a trailer pulled up into Ron's driveway. Then a machine started to make this loud noise, so loud you couldn't hear anything else. Art guessed, but he may be wrong, that the serviceman had come to flush out Ron's irrigation system in his back yard. It's like when people have to shut down their cottages for the winter. They drain all the pipes of water. Otherwise, when the temperature goes well below zero, a pipe may burst and a river start to flow through the cottage! This system is so neat. Underground hoses supply water to a sprinkler system. Ron turns on a knob and ... *bingo!* The grass lawns are watered.

I spent over an hour outside with Helen. The wind was cool but the sun was warm on my face. Helen did most of the digging up of carrots in that last garden by the raspberries. The carrots were smaller than the ones from the earlier garden by Ron's fence. Helen told me that this garden was a second planting. If it was a second planting, what happened to the first planting? She read my mind again, Mum. She seeded carrots early in May, and as soon as the seeds sprouted, birds came and ate every one of them except one that ended up growing all by itself until Helen planted the second group of seeds. Those birds included robins and crows migrating to Northern Ontario. Because it was now later in the season, the second planting of carrots did germinate, but the weather was not as warm and sunny later on, so the carrots couldn't grow large. It's that Daylight Savings Time coming to an end that messed up things.

I laughed when Helen told me a true story that happened when they lived in the country. It was late fall, and all kinds of birds were migrating south from Northern Ontario. Many stopped on their property to fill up for the long trek south. Robins in particular loved the red berries from this old mountain ash tree, and this day about a dozen or so stopped and started eating these delicious berries. Well, by evening when Helen looked out, she could see quite a few birds staggering like drunkards. Trying to stay upright was out of the question. Fermentation had occurred, and those berries were like alcohol in their little bellies. Thankfully by the next day their hangovers were gone and they continued on their long journey south. I hope they got their direction right. As you know, when someone is intoxicated, they don't know their right foot from their left!

Kane, a black dog similar to one that Helen and Art had, came walking by as Helen was still digging out carrots. He was a strong and energetic dog. His mom didn't let him come too close to the fence line. He wanted to go nose to nose with me, but I was on the other side of the fence. I felt safe with Helen there. Maybe Helen would bring out a magic corn broom again if Kane decided to do something weird! After a bit of a chit chat, the owner and Kane left for their daily one-hour-long walk.

When Art came out to help carry the carrots into the garage, a stranger came up the sidewalk and asked Art if he had seen a black Lab. Neither Helen nor Art had. They would see one if it was running around without its owner. This man had lost his dog. This is the second dog that has gone missing from this neighbourhood since I have come here.

Art's walk took me to the wetlands park. He had brought Helen's camera and took quite a few pictures. I guess they want a reminder of the happy times we've had together. It has been fun, Mum. After coming back home, Art had a cup of tea and some sort of square. I quickly positioned myself at his feet. He looked at me and spoke very slowly and clearly and told me I was not to have any chocolate, which was in the square of gluten free, egg free batter. He also told me not to ask for one crumb. To show that I understood every word, I went and lay down on the sofa. I think my vocabulary has expanded while being here, and I have learned what certain words in certain tones mean.

Before we came inside from our walk, a lady stopped to speak with us. Her name was Nina. She was so kind. She told Art that she and her husband have been living in a nearby condo, beside that forest, for three years. That is the same number of years Helen and Art have lived on Dowden. She told us that her daughter takes in rescue dogs too, just like Helen and Art used to. Those kinds of people are a special breed, Mum. Let us hope those two dogs that went missing in West Brant will find good homes.

Art phoned several organizations in hopes of getting rid of his older TV. No luck yet. We stopped at the plaza and spoke to a few boys who were gathered there. One said he would take it and would come here after school was out. He had been told to be here before 6:00 p.m. Well, he never showed up. He never phoned. He never came over to say that he had changed his mind. The art of communication and conversation is taking a spiral downward slump in that generation. They still have the old TV.

I was thirsty when we got back to Art's, and I headed straight to the water bowl. I have really appreciated the fresh water the Pasanens made available to me. We couldn't live long without water, could we, Mum? It's probably the most precious molecule of life on earth and beyond!

Art has collected a lot of verses from the Holy Bible pertaining to water, vapour, and rain, as he is trying to connect it to how the Holy Spirit operates in our lives. Whether that includes dogs, I don't know. Art has also collected data from scientific sources. He has named his project "Reflections on Water" for now. He's still waiting for a breakthrough, as there is still an element of revelation God has not shown him so that he can connect the "natural" with the "supernatural" realm. This is way beyond my thinking. Deep stuff, Mum.

Helen said that Henry David Thoreau (1817–1862) said, "Water is the only drink for a wise man." Where did he draw his conclusion from? What did he know that I do not know? I can just hear Helen saying, "Research it, Teddy!" Doctors who have written on the topic of diabetes will often devote a whole chapter on the importance of drinking water, because they know that water reduces inflammation and toxins that are the culprits in all kinds of diseases. Since your physical body is almost 70 per cent water, let us become wise persons and dogs by drinking not only physical water but water from the wells of salvation as found in God's Holy Word. Cheers, Mum!

I've reflected on many things while here on Dowden Avenue … the education and love I have received. I looked at Helen and rolled over on my back. She knew what that meant. She rubbed my tummy and thanked me for the memories and commented on my behaviour. She also said, "Thanks for being you, Teddy. It's been a pleasure caring for you."

Well, Mum, it is 6:08 p.m., and I think by now you're flying over Canadian land. I hope your flight is going smoothly. I have eaten my dinner and look forward to having whatever Helen is baking in the oven. I didn't see what she put into the pans, as I was exhausted and flaked out like a baby on the couch in the living room.

I think I will end my journaling now. Helen promises to make a copy for you. Tomorrow you can lift your feet up, nestle close to me, and read all about my adventures here at Dowden Avenue. I will be so happy to see you. Hundreds of hugs and kisses.

Yours eternally, Teddy. OX OX OX OX OX etc.

Conclusion
by Author
Helen S. Pasanen

I received great enjoyment from putting down on paper the streams of thoughts that contributed to *Teddy's Dog Diary*. I often laughed out loud as I questioned, "Could Teddy really be thinking this deeply?" Over the many years of taking in rescue dogs, I have come to appreciate the responsibility we have toward our furry companions, our friends, and the unconditional love they display when they know they are accepted and loved in a sea of humanity. That's not to say we should worship them, but we should lovingly care for them and diligently try to understand what they wish to convey to us.

Living a life that is God-pleasing includes how well we conduct the stewardship of our pets. As there are physical laws, there are spiritual laws to follow so that "peace" can prevail in all our relationships, including those with pets and life in general.

Our learning and our maturity hinges on our own attitudes toward life, God, our ambitions, our purposes, our relationships, and even our fears. There is power in expression. So often Teddy would express himself through his communicative barking, his eyes, his stance, or his body language. People express themselves similarly, but our natural selfish tendency as humans is to ignore the expressions, impressions, and thoughts coming at us. Our fine tuning to the needs of our pets and even friends diminishes, and our "moment of experience" vaporizes and is gone.

Life on earth is full of so many opportunities that slip through our fingers because we choose not to be in tune with our thoughts, emotions, or the vibrations of this created world. May I suggest, as I did so many times to Teddy, to "do some research," especially in Bible-based scriptures, and be transported into the variations of life surrounding you. Do not pass by the opportunities, as they are for a God-given purpose. In so doing, you may have a "diary" inside of you waiting to be released for the benefit of humanity!

Helen S. Pasanen

Other Books by Helen S. Pasanen

Journeys to Unknown Spiritual Frontiers—published by Word Alive Press
ISBN: 978-1-4866-1653-4

Listen, God is Calling—published by Word Alive Press
ISBN: 978-1-4866-1705-0

Each of these is available at Chapters/Indigo, Amazon, Word Alive Press, and Christian book stores.

Experiencing God at Grand Valley Christian Centre—printed by Minuteman Press, 40 Wellington Street North, Hamilton, Ontario, L8R 1M8

Available through the author or at Grand Valley Christian Centre, 379 Golf Road, Brantford, Ontario, N3T 5L8